VAMPIRES ARE FROM VENUS, WEREWOLVES ARE FROM MARS:
A Comprehensive Guide to Attracting Supernatural Love

(A Parody)

Vera Nazarian

ISBN-13: 978-1-60762-111-9
ISBN-10: 1-60762-111-8

Trade Paperback Edition

December 11, 2012

A Publication of
Norilana Books
P. O. Box 209
Highgate Center, VT 05459-0209
www.norilana.com

Published in the United States of America

Vampires are from Venus,
Werewolves are from Mars:

A Comprehensive Guide to Attracting Supernatural Love

Curiosities

an imprint of

Norilana Books

www.norilana.com

Other Books by Vera Nazarian

Lords of Rainbow
Dreams of the Compass Rose
Salt of the Air
The Perpetual Calendar of Inspiration
The Clock King and the Queen of the Hourglass
Mayhem at Grant-Williams High (YA)
The Duke in His Castle
After the Sundial

(Supernatural Jane Austen Series)

Mansfield Park and Mummies
Northanger Abbey and Angels and Dragons
Pride and Platypus: Mr. Darcy's Dreadful Secret

(Forthcoming)

Pagan Persuasion: All Olympus Descends on Regency

Cobweb Bride

Contents

Introduction

Congratulations! You've just stumbled upon the best-kept secret to social relationships.

Supernatural social relationships.

For years you've read *those books*, watched *those* movies and TV shows, surfed the shady gray fantasyscape of the internet, attended conventions full of highly intelligent people wearing highly constricting costumes.

You've even sat in prominent window seats at bookstore cafés pretending to write a *magnum opus* on your laptop while reading paranormal romance blogs—all in order to attract the precious attention of a *real* vampire, werewolf, fairy (sorry, *fae*), angel, demon, spotted hedgehog alien from another planet, or some other winged, horned, or tentacled supernatural lover.

Because it is a well-known fact they hang out at bookstore cafés. Or in alleys behind the cafés. Or deep in the sewers below the cafés. Or on rooftops above the cafés. . . .

Well, they *do*.

And always, they gaze at you from a distance. Not at the really more attractive person one table over, but at *you*—mousy, otherwise invisible you . . . watching you day and night.

They are watching you type on your laptop at that window. Watching you sip the mocha latte and wipe your mouth (and as you're at it, swipe your nose) with the napkin. Watching you absentmindedly chew, and often let bits of gooey crumb-cake rain down all over your shirt (because, yet again, you did not wear a bib—people your age do not wear a bib—even though you always later look back and think you kind of *should* wear a bib, as you spray the spot-cleaner detergent on the food stains at the laundry).

Ahem, and so—

Watching you, and waiting with intensity. With immortal longing. With smoldering eyes and chiseled lean cheekbones and artfully well-trimmed five-o-clock shadow scruff . . . all the while, swinging upside-down from the monkey bars of the fire escape of the building across the street from the café. . . .

At last! You're in luck!

This volume before you is *the definitive guide* to attracting that fascinating creature perched on the fire escape (or dangling from it), the supernatural soul mate of your dreams, no matter how they swing, or what planet they are from.

However—

Before we proceed, you must first figure out if *you yourself* are from a planet.

Yes, you've read that correctly.

When it comes to supernatural relationships, planets are a given. If you were dating an average, non-magical, random human fool, then there would be no mention of planets. None whatsoever. Okay, well, sometimes they mention planets, but not like this—and not like *all of them*.

But in this case, yes. We must invoke planets.

Because, really, you *need* to be grounded on some planet or another, not just freely orbiting a medium-class tiny yellow star in outer space.

You could be from just about anywhere—from Mars or Venus—or even Mercury, Jupiter, Saturn, Uranus, Neptune, Pluto, the Moon, the Oort Cloud, or hey, maybe even Earth (very rare).

In short, being planet-bound is a pre-requisite, in order to make the perfect paranormal match. Because, face it, no one wants to date someone who does *not* come from at least *some* tiny spinning ball in space. Even supernatural lovers with wings and jet propulsion capability like to rest on a rock now and then. Preferably, on a rock right next to you.

And so, we must now figure out your planet, and therefore, *you.*

Because what we're really talking about is your *soul planet*, the planet of your tendencies and dreams and desires and perfect love, not the actual physical rock on which you reside (Ahem, e-a-r-t-h.)

Soul-probing questions will be asked. You will respond.

Depending on your responses, you can then plan romantic dates, wedding venues, and the rest of your life (or undeath) accordingly.

Now—whether you're male or female—has nothing to do with any of this. There are plenty of metrosexual male denizens of Venus, and kickass females from Mars. So, gentlemen, please, flee not, and read on.

All right, you say.

What is my planet? What am I?

The only way to find out *what the dickens you are* is to take this **Universal, Absolutely Accurate, One Hundred Percent Infallible, Supernatural Personality And Compatibility Test**, or **UAAOHPISPACT**. (Yes, we tried to make the acronym have even more letters, but we failed, because we kept on forgetting which letters got used, which letters were next to each other, and which words came first, next, or last, and frankly, it kind of got out of control, so then we needed a drink. . . .)

Anyway, here is the sophisticated psychological analysis engine, the carefully crafted, deeply probing power tool of introspection and self-discovery that is the UAAOHPISPACT.

Take the multiple choice test by instinctively recognizing the best answer, but then for some reason choosing the not-so-best one, or even a really crappy one, the same way you selected that last date. (In your dreams! Like, you ever went on a real date! HAHAHAHAHA! And LOL and ROTFL and ROTFLMAO! Admit it, they were all just "Hey, did you eat yet? Let's go have lunch, okay?" things, and the other person had no clue you two were in fact sharing a Meal of Mating Significance. Ahem! Sorry. Okay, maybe you *have* gone out on dates—yes, even more than one—so, maybe it's just me. *Okay, putting down the martini now . . .*)

In other words, the results of your test answer selections are, well, as messed up (or not) as you are (or not).

Got that?

And now, grab a piece of paper and start writing down the letters. Or the answers. Or the letters of the answers to the letters.

Whatever. Just write some sh**—BLEEP! down.

Universal, Absolutely Accurate, One Hundred Percent Infallible, Supernatural Personality And Compatibility Test

Question 1

A) Should a vampire sparkle?

B) Should a werewolf sparkle?

C) Should you sparkle?

D) Beer.

(I realize this is more of a rhetorical question, or maybe less than a normal question, or possibly not really a question at all but a groaning multiple-choice moan against the big cold universe, but what the hell, just pick one. *I don't know what this is.* Just go with your gut. If your gut happens to be a beer gut, choose D.)

Question 2

If faced with a dark, mysterious, hot stranger at a party, do you:

A) Offer them your neck and phone number.

B) Tell them they smell nice but you are nobody's bitch.

C) Slowly back away and then get the heck out of there, then text all about it in the parking lot until they disable your account for spamming.

D) Try to stake them. With a chopstick. Or a ball-point pen. Or a porterhouse.

Question 3

This is the one movie you have seen one too many times. (Choose carefully, even if you have seen this movie only once).

A) Flashlight

B) Daylight

C) Nightlight

D) Searchlight

E) Pilot Light

Question 4

What's your dream partner's name?

A) Edmund

B) Jackson

C) Betta

D) Tuffy

E) Larry (Wait, what?)

F) Fredo (Woah!)

Question 5

If you put Edmund, Jackson, Betta, and Tuffy in one room, what happens?

A) Tuffy stakes Edmund . . . you know, with a *filet mignon.* Betta and Jackson ride off together on a scooter.

B) Tuffy makes out with Edmund (because Angle and

Spoke are not enough). Betta and Jackson ride off together on a segway.

C) Tuffy stakes Edmund . . . you know, with a rib-eye. Tuffy beats the crap out of Betta. Tuffy puts a collar and leash on Jackson and they go jogging.

D) Tuffy sees who's inside the room, tosses in a canister, lights a match and shuts the door. She takes a bus to Cleveland where there's another Smellmouth.

Question 6

You are going on a blind date. What do you wear?

A) Dark period clothing (what period exactly, is anyone's guess, but it's early Pre-Cell Phone Period), thick smoky eyeliner and "black-eye" eye shadow, anemia-mime makeup, blood-red lipstick that goes outside the line of your actual lips (you failed coloring books in kindergarten), leather corset, random vinyl embellishments, lace fingerless gloves (topped by pewter poison rings), prosthetic fangs, prosthetic mini-horns (tastefully dipped in black and burgundy glitter), hand-made steampunk jewelry from a trendy online boutique or purchased through a major online auction site where you scored it after a heated bidding war with a thirteen-year-old in another country.

B) Dog collar with big metal studs.

C) Jeans and t-shirt.

D) A Wedding gown or tux—why wait? You are about to meet the fairy (sorry, fae) of your dreams. And all stories insist that time itself moves differently in Faerie—a. k. a. Faerie Savings Time (FST). The closest we have to that is Microwave Time, which is almost as inexplicable and excruciating.

Question 7

You are giving a party. What's NOT on the menu?

A) The guests and the caterers.

B) Fat little children. What, you think this is Jonathan Swift?

C) The pizza delivery guy. And the pizza. *Especially* the pizza.

D) You.

Question 8

In a cage match, who would be the ultimate champion?

A) Vampire

B) Werewolf

C) Fairy (or Fae)

D) A high school girl with a wooden dowel sharpened on one end.

E) Armed Weapon of Mass Destruction. (Hint: see D)

Question 9

You want to settle down and have a family and a 30-year fixed mortgage. Whom do you date?

A) A sexy undead vampire who is 600 years old and has a mysterious Greco-Albanian accent, silk underwear, and a bloated bank account in every city and on every continent.

B) A gorgeous, buff, and tanned werewolf who is 27 years old and has a college loan, boxer briefs, a mysterious tattoo, and intricate family connections in Vegas and Monte Carlo.

C) A hot guy of indeterminate age who wears black leather and has a slight hump on his back—could be a gun holster, could be a pair of folded wings, could be an actual hump. No credit cards, but always carries unlimited wads of cash.

D) A hot female with a bow and arrows and a dystopian attitude. Has nothing except a small backpack and awesome target-practice skills.

E) A male or female geek (take your pick) who has invented a social network or an operating system while messing around with vacuum tubes and room-sized computers in college, and now runs a Fortune 500 company.

Question 10

Your parents are nagging you about being single. Where do you go to find your perfect romantic partner?

A) Graveyards, museums, blood drives, antique shops, cultural lectures, winery tours.

B) The zoo, or an exotic safari. Or, more likely, an animal rescue shelter, because you are underemployed.

C) Science fiction or comics (ahem, graphic novels!) conventions.

D) Online, because, where else?

Congratulations! You've completed all the multiple choice test questions! Hopefully you even wrote them down somewhere other than your palm.

Now, let's score and tabulate your answers and come up with the sickening moment of truth ... your personalized UAAOHPISPACT results. Your *soul planet* awaits!

Your Personalized UAAOHPISPACT Test Results

First, look at your answers. Yes, down there. No. THERE.

Found it? Do you need to squint? No? Good, you are sober enough. Or, at least you have your glasses on. Or your contacts. Disposable contacts (fancy schmancy, jeez! What a shi**—BLEEP!).

❖ If you have picked mostly "A" answers in the multiple choice, then you are naturally attracted to vampires. They are from Venus, and therefore you are a Venusian at heart. You might be a thoroughly human girl or boy living in Montebello, but deep inside, **Venusian**.

❖ If you have picked mostly "B" answers in the multiple choice, then you are naturally attracted to werewolves. They are from Mars, and therefore you are a **Martian** at heart.

❖ If you have picked mostly "C" answers in the multiple choice, then you are naturally attracted to fairies (or fae). They are from Mercury (if male) or the Moon (if female), and therefore you are a **Mercurian** or a **Moon-Lunarian**.

❖ If you have picked mostly "D" answers in the multiple choice, then you are naturally attracted to females with martial arts skills or metrosexual males. They are from Earth, and therefore you are an **Earthling** in both the real-world and soul sense. Congratulations! You're Almost Average ™!

❖ If you have picked mostly "E" answers in the multiple choice, then you have *not* answered all the questions. You think you can get away with anything. And yes, you are naturally attracted to yourself, or to rotting zombies. They—and you—are from Jupiter (also a bloated giant), and therefore you are a **Jupiterian**.

❖ If you have picked mostly "F" answers in the multiple choice, then you have answered only *one* of the questions, which makes you scary-fixated on one thing only, in the intense way of an Ancient Egyptian Mummy looking for its long-lost love. And yes, you are attracted to hairy feet in a bucolic countryside. They (mummies *and* hairy feet) are from Neptune (if female) or Saturn (if male), and therefore you are a **Neptunian** or **Saturnian**.

❖ If you have picked a more-or-less even mix of "A, B, C, D, E, and F" answers in the multiple choice, then you are either well balanced or very conflicted and moderately confused, in the bad-boy (or girl) way of a hell-spawn demon. Which means that you are either an asshole or tend to look up your own asshole a lot. The answers are not there, but oh, so many spinning rings! They (demons *and* rings) are from Uranus, and therefore you are a **Uranusian**.

❖ If you have picked any other uneven combination or frequency of "A, B, C, D, E, or F" answers in the multiple choice, then frankly you are either from the Asteroid Belt, the Oort Cloud, or from Pluto (which was recently demoted from full-fledged planethood, so gets stuck in this asteroidal bunk-bed category), and therefore, you, my friend, are the *unknown*, the wild card, the x solved for y, the raging wilderness, the oddball in all of this! Feel free to follow your heart whichever way it leads in the supernatural romantic partner aspect. Date a unicorn, for all we care, don't let anyone stop you! Be aware however, that relativistic ghosts and spirits, not to mention winged angels, are all around you! This of course makes you, in the neither-here-nor-there sense, a **Quantum Planetoid**.

How to Read and Interpret Your Results

Now that we've established *what the dickens you are*, it's time to match you up with your romantic partner and supernatural soul mate!

First, a round of cosmic laughter.

Next, we throw the results of the UAAOHPISPACT out the window.

Yeah, you are getting the picture now. Because, all this supernatural matchmaking sh**—BLEEP! is infinitely more difficult than you think. *No one* ever listens to the matchmaker. No one.

You might think that now that you know your *soul planet*, you immediately know your supernatural soul mate.

You might *think* that Venusians go well together with other Venusians, or Martians go well with other Martians, etc. Wow, have you got it all wrong!

Well then, you might think that maybe Venusians go

well together with Martians? Kind of in the way of caramel and chocolate?

BUZZZT! Wow, that's *really* wrong. So woefully horrendously wrong. So wrong that *it's actually an exception to all the supernatural rules of compatibility and attraction.*

Because those two go together like eggs and burning asphalt. Or rubber tires and cauliflower. They also frequently go *at* each other—to kill, maim, tear each other to bits, eviscerate, decimate, and do bad, bad things to each other's electronics, personal belongings, and underwear. Do not, under any circumstances, leave a Venusian and a Martian in the same room unsupervised, unless you plan a remodel and want to save on demolition expenses.

However—any other planetary combinations can be mixed and matched liberally without any remorse or regret, only sheer romantic delight.

Truth is, it's a mix-and-match kind of universe. A universe in which vampires, werewolves, fairies (fae, dammit!!!), zombies, mummies, demons, ghosts, angels, random unclassified inter-dimensional alien sea monsters, and ordinary human bumpkins are all in the same dating pool (Manhattan is a good cross-sample, but London, Paris, Moscow, Tokyo, Atlanta, Lubbock, Fresno, Watsonville, or Bakersfield, all work just as well).

If you are Venusian, sticking your eager neck out for every hottie with fangs, the last thing you need is an *actual* vampiric immortal leach in your life. You need someone who can understand your foolish need to be sucked dry and instead can provide you with a means of restraint and some vitamin and iron supplements.

If you are a Martian with a passion for rough play, for furry and fiery slobbering and wild kingdom claw scratches, what you really need is a calm, genteel, and mummified soul mate to fall back upon. Because falling down, rolling over, and playing dead is something you do well, and a nice calcified shoulder of support is just the thing needed to break your downfall.

And so on, and so forth. Know and remember the *secret formula* of supernatural attraction—*opposites attract* (with the caveat of vampires and werewolves—separate them immediately).

They really do. Not because they aren't so damn annoying when you first encounter them (they are). But because, to each other, they—well—*sparkle*.

At least, in your poor impressionable mind they do. First, they sparkle with that aggravating, uppity, know-it-all asshole one-upmanship. Next, they glitter with a kind of perverse slow-burn angel hotness. And finally—with all those fireworks and sparks and *alchemical* chain reactions and organic *chemistry* happening between the two of you—you're mesmerized, enchanted, stunned, and absolutely terminally hooked. And, for one brief shining moment, you suddenly *understand math.*

You are *in supernatural love.*

Or at least you think you are. Because, to be honest, you still have no clue.

Yes, it's a scary big universal dating pool.

We all have to get along, so we are all naturally attracted to people with whom we *must learn* to get along.

Because, at the end of the cosmic day (and just before cosmic happy hour), we kind of need them. And they need us. So that the world does not fall apart as a result of our infantile unresolved conflict. Because what comes next is global climate change, some kind of *fluctuating barometric pressure* (what that means exactly, no one is sure, but it sounds frightening), funky-socks atmosphere, rising sea levels, everyone packing into the international space station, and anti-gravity underwear. (Oh, and don't forget the magnetic poles flipping. Our tablets and smart phones all stop working, *all our digital content disappears forever*—bite your tongue!—and we might as well lie down and die, surrounded by cats.)

All the more reason to get hooked up with a supernatural soul mate, pronto.

Notice how the metrosexual-but-manly vampire pines for the bland and spineless human girl with an unusual amount of missing personal attributes, who pines back (and also sort of pines on the side, for the furry hot-blooded werewolf)? Notice how the fairy (argh, fae, *fae!*) princess loves the thoroughly human boy? How the street-tough girl with untapped paranormal powers loves to beat up on a delicate fanged bloodsucker in a black cape, or to torment the furry man-toy detective who follows her around like a puppy, thinking that she is either a mysterious demon in disguise or just a real hot bitch?

Yes, the examples are varied and plentiful, and uniformly make no rational sense. And yet they all point to one thing—the love matches are as complicated and as enticing as anything in your wildest imagination, and again, *opposites attract*. As a mushroom craves moonlight, so does a boring human lust for her vampire.

So, without further ado, time to sort this whole supernatural lover thing out! Let's resort to pointedly pointless and pointy detailed analysis.

Venus—Your Vampire Lover

What is it that makes the *vampire lover* the crème de la crème, the paragon ideal, the superstar placed firmly at the top of the paranormal romantic hierarchy? Why oh why, Lord? Why oh why, oh-woe-to-us why?

Are we really so much into cold clammy skin? Is chronic anemia a turn-on? And what's with all this immortal necrophilia?

Used to be, vampires were truly frightening, frequently bald, icky rotten-corpse monsters with long teeth and skeletal claws, that rise up every night from the dirt-packed (and surprisingly three-way adjustable) grave and suck your blood, draining you dry. This either turns you into a monster too, or else you just die. Eeow!

But now, all of a sudden, they are dreamboat hunks!

Seriously, how did this sh**—BLEEP! happen?

How did all those vampires become pretty sissies and take over popular literature and entertainment, and propagate in our common consciousness and our bookstore cafés, breeding like undead grave-dust-bunnies, and mutating virally into the immortal cholera of our darkest romantic dreams?

Vampires are tall, dark, and doornail-*dead*. And now, they are fu*****—BLEEP! everywhere!

So many questions. So much that makes you want to say very naughty words and throw things. So little that makes sense.

Fu*****—BLEEP! sh**—BLEEP! BLEEP! Twi*****—BLEEP! BLEEP! BLEEP!

And speaking of not making sense—let's get right to it. Venus is the second planet from the sun, boiling-hot and roiling with primeval gases, especially methane (think, auto exhaust and farts). Naturally, it is the planet of Love. And naturally it is associated with clammy, cold, undead hunks. Because love is a paradox, you know. Hot is cold, and wet is dry, and weak is strong, and dead is intense.

Venus is also related to veins. And you know, blood. Venus is thus the essence of vampires, and those of us who are permeated with it are the Venusians.

What does it mean to be Venusian? An immortal need to *think* you need to suck blood and scowl romantically in the moonlight? An automatic endowment of good looks and manual dexterity? The ability to fly without a four-hour airport delay and turn into a fruit bat? (Wait, is it the other kind of bat?)

Not at all. It merely means that *you are obsessed with vampires*. You don't actually need or want them, you only think you do. And, it also means that occasional vampires are obsessed with you (you hope—see, there goes that pesky obsession, rearing its psycho head!).

Still expect to make any sense from any of this? Still struggling to find meaning in a cold sucking void of immortal ennui?

Voila! You so nailed this coffin. You are so Venusian. There is no sense to be had, at least not in your headspace.

Now, stop it! What you need is a proper supernatural mate to snap you the hell out of it.

Ideal Mate for a Venusian

Your ideal mate is *anyone who is not a vampire.* Seriously. Just anyone. Please, date a tub of ice cream or a bag of chips, and you will do better in the long run.

However, werewolves, and hence **Martians** are *not* recommended.

But a nice human co-worker will be just perfect for you. You need an **Earthling**, and stat! Set that alarm clock to some morning hour (hint, before 2:00 PM), leave your cat on your pillow, step out into the sun, and enjoy your real planet!

Mars—Your Werewolf Lover

Werewolves are almost as bad as vamps. They used to be so disgusting. So scary-hairy, so fur-covered. . . . Basically, gruesome monster beasts of vaguely wolf-human shape, with big teeth and claws and horrifying burning red eyes— and not just in undoctored photographs. They used to be overgrown, slobbering canines, at best. They used to eat little girls in red riding hoods. And yes, they used to be distinctly gross, and occasionally sorry and pitiful in the way you feel sorry for any mangy wolf or dog, even the demonic rabid kind.

But suddenly they are hot hunks. And not just any hunks, but *hunks without any hint of body hair!* Hunks with perfectly shaved chests and defined six-pack abs of kitchen appliance-grade stainless steel, and well-placed tattoos, and yummy biceps and triceps and . . . ahem. It's as if they figured out how to supernaturally retract their hair back *up* the follicles, tastefully hide it, keeping all of it in reserve (in another dimension? In Vegas? In area rugs?), until they are overcome with crazy hair-growth pressure every month. . . . So that when the moon is full, they exhale in relief, put away the razors, hot wax, and depilatory supplies, and *just let themselves go*. All to hell. . . .

The wolf shape-shifter has become a paragon of the fiery and virile male. They are hot-blooded, and in general, kind of crazy-hot in every sense. And girl-werewolves are the vixens (pardon the vaguely canine pun) that are legendary for being fierce warriors between the sheets (no, really, they fire automatic weapons at pillows and chew the crap out of the mattress).

And naturally, these animal magnetism-imbued werewolves are associated with Mars, the distant, absolutely frigid, freezing-cold planet, orangey-red in color because of rust and iron ore deposits, and very, very far away. Mars is the planet of War—and that's even outside the bedroom. Everybody knows war is hot. And cold. While peace, or even *détente,* sucks (like a vampire) for the individual and the economy. Makes perfect sense.

Anyway, what does it mean to be Martian?

First of all, it means, you're a dog person. Also, *you are obsessed with werewolves*. You stopped shaving. And you think that it might be fun to run around crazy-naked once a month in the moonlight, roll in the wet grass, run through sprinklers, and then TP someone's house.

Honest, you don't *really* want to hurt or tear apart anyone with your teeth, human or not. And you really wouldn't want to hurt that poor bunny in the bushes! At best you might fantasize how you *might* pull your nails against your lover's back and then make extra-loud exaggerated panting noises. Lovemaking to you is not an art but a sorority-on-frat party.

Things for you are either fun or crazy, and things are

pretty simple. Life's okay, as long as you've got comfort stuff. And weekends. And as long as you have someone warm to love, and who unconditionally loves you back.

And that's all it comes down to. Warmth. (Because, remember, real Mars is so damn cold.)

Ideal Mate for a Martian

You don't want another hungry wolf in your life. You don't want someone to take you apart on a daily basis, and to rob you of your will to live and your electronic gadgets. You want warm soothing comfort, and a lot of hearty food and passionate noises. Stuff that basically tells you that you're *alive*, and so is the supernatural lover of your dreams.

For that reason, ghosts and hence **Quantum Planetoids** are *not* recommended.

Neither are zombies and hence **Jupiterians**, because you don't want a bloated egoist self-lover for a soul mate (and besides you have plenty of your own hot air).

Vampires and therefore **Venusians** are a big flaming no-no.

Demon **Uranusians**, a.k.a., assholes, are just not good for you, since they encourage the crazy in you, make you go out and do bad things, and you are so susceptible to naughty temptation and infomercials.

Mummies are a mixed bag, being dead, but kind of sweet in a desiccated romantic sense. So take your chance with a **Neptunian** or **Saturnian** but be very careful not to dry up yourself.

Earthlings are generally okay, and can be a solid good match. They will reliably lock you up during the full moon, cutely calling it "the fool moon!" And the rest of the time you will just be two people basking in ordinary love and regularly eating greasy spoon diner food.

However, your best bet is an immortal fairy (or, *pardon* me, fae) who can keep their cool while you rave and slobber (because you do, a whole lot, especially after you've had cookies or ice cream or a chili-burger), and who will match your repressed needs, fury, jealous fits, and stalker tendencies, with a no-nonsense steady affection and soothing music of the spheres that will turn you into a happy puppy. Therefore, go look for that **Mercurian** or **Moon-Lunarian** of your hottest supernatural dreams!

Mercury and Moon—Your Fairy (Fae) Lover

Admit it, fairies—or fae—are very hot right now. They've been around (and hot) for almost as long as the vampires, and quite frankly, longer. But even though they are just as beautiful and attractive and immortal and metrosexual, and yes, dangerous, for some reason they've paled in comparison to the even more pale bloodsuckers.

It has to be the blood. Or the erotic neck-biting thing.

Whatever the reason, fairies (or fae—oh, for crissake! Can I just pick one or the other for the rest of this thing? No? Would it be offensive? Okay, no) are just not as interesting in the eyes of the public. For some reason— maybe because they are so darn mysterious, and no one understands exactly their magical origins—we tend to relegate them to the background.

Or—is it actual faerie (fae? fey? Aaaargh!) magic?

Are they doing this, *right now?* Right this instant? Putting on a fairy-fae glamour on us so that we can only see them out of the corner of our eye? Or so that we barely manage to even *think* of them . . . and only after we kinda-sorta make a major effort to remember that they're even *there*, and they are so infinitely more hot and desirable than vampires?

After all, just think: faeries are usually highly eligible, single blue-bloods, royalty, princes and princesses and kings and queens of some mysterious otherworldly kingdoms, while vampires don't even have their own blood and have to take other people's. And they rule a crummy nightclub or two, and mostly the underground sewers.

Fairies are immortal and alive. Vampires have to die first before they become immortal, and then they are dead, or "undead." (What in blazes is "undead?" Some freaky in-between state between life and whatever the heck the *other thing* is? It is seriously messed up, if you ask me. . . . HIC!)

Fae have supernatural powers of the mind, and super strength, and mad-skillz musical ability and heavenly voices not requiring digital enhancement. In contrast, with all their fancy telepathy and eyeball hypnotism, no one has heard a vampire sing, and most of them don't even breathe or collapse their lungs, unless they concentrate very, very hard. Ever seen a vamp play a tenor sax? Exactly. And, guess who invented lip sync? Yeah.

So really, at last the secret is out!

Faerie-fae-fairy-fey are quite intentionally making themselves *less attractive* to us, compared to vampires, so that they can be all sneaky in the background of the world.

Damn, but they're good!

Admittedly, they can be cruel and mean and terrifying too, but what godlike paragon isn't? After all, the Moon is tiny in the greater scheme of planet things, but it's huge and devastating in our poetic imagination—deceptively cool and stately-slow, sailing in the night heavens—and it controls the tides. And Mercury is also tiny, scalding-hot on one side only (like your toast), and super-fast, and closest to the sun and far from us—and yet it has that damned Retrograde every few months that causes our mail to get lost, our pants to shrink in the dryer, and ruins our travel plans. How is that not sneaky and impressive?

So, what does it mean to be a Mercurian or Moon-Lunarian?

It means that *you are obsessed with androgynous beauty and immortality*, and you very likely think you're a Venusian, when in fact you would much rather have the *living* flesh-and-blue-blood immortal than the undead, and all you need is someone to slap you upside the head a few times and clean your foggy glasses.

Open your eyes, forget the bloody bloodsucker, and see the sexy supernatural wonders of Faerie all around you!

Or else, you already *know* all this (sneaky fae-fairy you!). And you already see, and breathe the magic. In that case, carry on!

Ideal Mate for a Mercurian or Moon-Lunarian

The fae are remarkably beautiful, aesthetically perfect in every way, proud and hot, and occasionally sadistic. So unless you are an absolute clod, you will probably be able to attract a remarkable variety of sensible and romantic supernatural partners, as long as they are supermodel-perfect.

Zombies and hence **Jupiterians** are emphatically *not* recommended.

Neptunian or **Saturnian** mummies are a long stretch, because of oily flapping bits of rag and sailor-windblown dry skin. But the *inner* beauty of their loyal romantic souls can go a long way when propped up against mere dermatology.

As always, **Earthlings** are something to fall back upon, though there may be some time-based confusion, what with all that Faerie Savings Time™ versus Daylight Savings.

However, the most delightful mates for you are made of thin air. Ghostly and angelic **Quantum Planetoids** can be an ethereal good bet. So go outside and let the wind blow the two of you together, and let the Aeolian Harp sing!

Earth—Your Almost Average™ or Androgynous Power Human Lover

Ah, Earthlings. My dear, oh-so-boring Earthlings. You are mundane, ordinary, grounded on a rock in every sense of the word, aspiring to heights measured in inches rather than feet (convert to appropriate metric, if applicable, dear rest of the world).

Your greatest excitement is evoked by hybrid car mileage. And your idea of a supernatural lover is someone who knows Kung Fu, understands Algebra, or is vegetarian (that's so fairy, you think).

The distant lure of beautiful immortality and blood-sucking good looks touches you with the force of a distant gentle breeze. In other words, you sort of enjoy all that paranormal stuff, and you even watch that spook channel on a regular basis.

But when it comes down to it, it's never the hot

vampire or smoldering werewolf that catches your attention, but the kickass female or the hunky human detective male that interacts with them.

You are incorrigible in your delight with the young and the pretty (or at least androgynous) heroes and heroines, whose achievements could place them in the Olympics. But that's as far as you are willing to go to stretch your inner wings and your love muscle (the inner metaphorical kind—eeow, what did you think I was saying? Jeez, BLEEP!).

What does it mean to be an Earthling?

It means you are at least aware of other (non-Earthling) possibilities, but are *obsessed with human action*—movies and TV, and are likely into spectator sports, medieval reenactments, boy bands (or one-girl-surrounded-by-boys bands), and have a calendar on your wall with someone's bodacious picture (or as your screensaver or background pic).

Ideal Mate for an Earthling

At your supernatural best, you will do very well with other **Earthlings**.

However, in recent years you have revealed a somewhat inexplicable love for zombies and hence **Jupiterians**. It's definitely not something to be proud of, or encouraged, since animated rotting corpses are about as sexy as, well, rotting corpses. Naturally you say you don't want to date them, only blow their brains out, from the comfortable distance of your gaming console. But really, we all know that's just your kind of action foreplay. So go ahead, blow off a little steam (and gray matter, theirs and your own). And then, please, try another less repulsive supernatural obsession.

Another hopeless attraction for you is a demon lover asshole also known as a **Uranusian**. You tend to mistake demons for people who know Kung Fu (or for people who *think* they know Kung Fu), so before you get yourself in too deep, or sign any contract in blood and brimstone (disguised as a sub-prime mortgage refinance loan), just cool it, okay? Go out on a date or two, and see the asshole for what they really are—a person circling their own inner drain.

As a good match instead, you are recommended a **Mercurian** or **Moon-Lunarian**, because they are light as air, wise and cool, and can teach you to cast away mortal dullness, TV remote controls, earthly gravity, and then to lift off and fly. And **Quantum Planetoids** are recommended for a similar reason, because ghosts and angel wings can lift you up and widen your mind beyond the cable channel lineup.

Don't be afraid to try something even *more* supernatural than you *think* you like!

Jupiter—Self Love or Your Zombie Lover

Oh dear. Here we go. At last, it's all about *YOU*. Yes, you with capital letters and bloated head.

Is there anything more oversized than Jupiter, belching primordial fart gases, hosting a permanent storm "spot" the size of a galactic elephant on one humongous hemisphere, being entirely inhospitable not only to life but to, well, having an actual surface to walk on, and having less overall density then a desert sand storm, not to mention being foul-rotting and undead?

The answer is, you.

That's right, you zombie slow-moving, self-loving Jupiterian, your excesses, demands, and liquefied dripping brains know no bounds. Your notion of romance is a mirror and a box of erotic products in discreet brown packaging. And brains. Anyone's brains.

How did zombies get so popular with the rest of us? They are filthy rotting meat sacks. They are animated corpses with exposed bones, decaying limbs and slime. They move with jerks, using malfunctioning body parts. And if they bite you, you are screwed, because they virally transmit their zombie condition to you until you yourself collapse, die, then "wake up" and rot. Good thing they are usually slower than a granny at the supermarket. Gives you (ahem, other people, since the "you" being discussed here is the Jupiterian zombie) plenty of time to escape.

Zombies also mill around like moo-cows. And if they go anywhere, they usually travel in mobs of infected individuals. Let's call 'em z-mobs. You know how that works—a pride of lions, a murder of crows, a z-mob of zombies. Normally, supernatural lovers tend to be loners, and no other supernatural entity is into flash mobs to that extent. Especially not such *lame* flash mobs—totally without synchronized choreography or dance moves, and with only humming grunts and moans in place of a perky techno music track. A z-mob will surround and overpower you by their sheer numbers, crush and then tear you apart from limb to limb. And a single zombie will feed on you exactly the same way, only take way longer.

So what does it mean to be a Jupiterian?

Well, for starters, you have a very messed up self-image. And—in a perfect example of what psychologists refer to as *transference*—you are *obsessed with relocating all your non-admitted faults from yourself to an outside object*, which takes on the form of a filthy rotting zombie. It's kind of like that proverbial hidden portrait in the attic that grows hideous, old, and ugly from evil deeds, while the subject remains young and beautiful. Except, instead of a portrait, you transfer your interior crap onto zombies. That way you can hate those very things about yourself from a safe distance, and even use them for target practice. Blast those zombies, baby! And all the while, continue to tell yourself you are "hot stuff."

Ideal Mate for a Jupiterian

It's easy to just say that an ideal mate for someone with this bloated condition is yourself. However, that's just idiotic. Put two Jupiterians together and they will never ever *never ever* NEVER mate. They will just sit in different corners and pretend the other bloated giant is not present, while they blast away at rubbish from their gaming consoles.

A fairy (fae) **Mercurian** or **Moon-Lunarian** is not a good match, because fae are just too prissy to deal with ugly zombie messes, and they will not suffer a fool with liquefied brains.

Neither is an angelic or ghostly **Quantum Planetoid** a particularly good choice—though not for lack of trying. Oh, those infinitely patient, sweet angel creatures will flit and blow about and try to make a difference in your futile existence, but there is just *no saving* a zombie. Seriously, just too much rot.

Neptunian or **Saturnian** mummies are equally useless, and at best will be simply ignored by the potential zombie lover, or at worst taken for furniture.

Werewolves and hence **Martians** are *not* recommended, since they will only make matters worse for the meaty bag that is our zombie, by mistaking them for freshly killed meat and trying to eat them. Not too bright, and—Ugh!

In the opposite direction, **Earthlings** are also horrible matches, because a zombie will immediately smell fresh living brains and want to eat *them* in turn. Run, Earthling, just run! (And don't mock their determined-but-lurching slow approach by whooping, sticking your tongue out while making googly cross-eyes, and chicken-flapping your arms at them. Because, naturally you will trip, get pinned by fallen furniture, and things will then take a grim and rapid downturn . . .)

So, what's the supernatural soul mate solution for these nearly helpless cases?

Prepare to be amazed.

The one and only time that we can recommend a **Venusian** to anyone, is in this case. Yes, believe it or not, a hoity toity image-conscious, trendy vampire is an excellent role model for a rotting slob zombie lover. An elegant vampire will quickly relate to their deeply hidden internal angst—after all, both are undead corpses, liable to rot (ahem, we shall not *speak* of that). A vampire knows exactly what that's like. But a vampire will *not* tolerate that kind of unaesthetic ickiness for even a moment, and all gooey rot will be immediately disguised, modified, cosmetically hidden via metaphysical liposuction. Therefore, the zombie will find itself suddenly feeling much prettier, in control of its eternally decaying and collapsing body, and able to somehow get their sh**— BLEEP! together already.

Before you know it, a zombie will stop milling in place, pull in its gut (literally, intestines will have to be stuffed back into the abdominal cavity), put on dramatic makeup, and slightly deflate, both in ego and pressurized gases. This is what happens when you find the perfect supernatural soul mate!

Neptune and Saturn—Your Mummified Object of Fixation or Stalker Mummy Lover

Being a mummy is such a distinguished undead tradition, filled with colorful history, pointy pyramids, golden treasure, mysterious tombs, dashing archeologists, dramatic curses, and tragic star-crossed lovers.

No other monster is so versatile as the long-suffering and under-appreciated noble mummy. Who else can be *tragic, terrifying, romantic,* and *funny,* all at the same time?

Consider this—a mummy is often a noble ancient pharaoh or queen who dies tragically, usually involving their lovely bride or handsome groom in some kind of suicide pact or outright murder (think, jealousy, or treachery), and gets magically cursed, and then gets to be mummified (eeow, don't even ask—natron salts and organ removal and oily rags are involved, and you are basically pickled), wrapped in what looks like toilet paper, is placed in a golden box, and then it dries out for many thousands of years, as it lies there, waiting, waiting, waiting. . . . The poor mummy is waiting to re-start its life again, and to find its long-lost love, and to maybe take revenge against the bad people who ruined its life. Instead, the mummy gets to be chased by ensemble comedy teams in summer blockbuster movie franchises, or stuck in Jane Austen parody mash-up novels. And it never gets the girl (or boy).

Talk about complex and conflicted! Sad and funny! Ridiculous and sublime!

Saturn is the grim, big, dark, gloomy pessimistic taskmaster planet of no weekends and icy undefined atmosphere. And that's just at the office. It has even bigger rings than Uranus, but remains utterly humorless. Neptune is very similar, and much farther out there, a verifiable space cadet, with not too much known about it material makeup. Both are large, gaseous, low-density, stoic, and eternally inhospitable venomous iceboxes.

So what does it mean to be a Neptunian or Saturnian?

As a loyal and mummified undead dreamer, *you are obsessed with immortal true love*, and will wait for as long as it takes. Unfortunately it may literally take forever.

Poor, stoic Neptune girl and Saturn boy, sometimes it seems you must have been born on a Wednesday. No matter how much you watch and wait and follow and, ahem, *stalk* your subject of affection in a distant long-orbit holding pattern, nothing seems to be working.

Ideal Mate for a Neptunian or Saturnian

Because the mummy-inspired persons are so loyal and willing to wait, and to work so darn hard to attain their perfect supernatural soul mate, their choices are both very narrow and also rather unlimited. Tada! A paradox.

Neptunians or Saturnians either wait for the right one, or settle for the first one. And that "first one" is usually the first supernatural potential lover in your circle of acquaintances who actually stops long enough to pay attention to you, recognizing for once that you are a mummy and not a piece of antique furniture. What choice do you make? Do you take their hand, or do you retreat into that comfy and safe sarcophagus?

How very perverse indeed.

But let's be optimistic. Supposing that a mummy does *not* have to settle, what else is there (besides a restraining order)?

A **Martian** werewolf is likely to rip into your rag-and-toilet-paper getup and gnaw your crunchy old bones. So, *not* recommended.

A demonic obnoxious **Uranusian** is going to really hold you back (and down) in your personal eternity, and keep you in the nether regions of the afterlife, at the gates of hell, Canoga Park, or Pacoima. Stay away from the assholes!

An **Earthling**—usually that very same long-lost lover of your grave dreams—will simply break your heart. Trust me on this, you will *never* get them to "enter eternity with you," no matter how well you sell it, or how romantic you are as you beg and plead. Besides, they usually have another living flesh-and-blood Earthling lover already lined up, so you are just an odd third. Yes, it's sad, but it is also practical. So, just don't even bother. Have a good cry, in the metaphorical sense (sans tears: you have no water on you, nor eyeballs, nor tear ducts, remember . . . and for that matter, you may not even have a properly attached head), and then just move on.

Most other supernaturals we will not even bother to mention to you—they are the ones who see you as furniture. You are not a loveseat, so, moving right along . . .

Your real and best love match is with a gentle **Quantum Planetoid**, the angel sucker for lost causes, the fellow ghost haunted by their past lives. Together you can haunt ancient places, and remember, and wait for something fair and just, and contemplate the true nature of immortal love. This is kind of very beautiful, and I am getting teary-eyed, because you two will at last be in a better place, voluntarily, and *two shall become one*.

Uranus—Your Asshole Demon Lover

Here is another inexplicable modern cultural dreamboat—a sexy red-hot bad boy (or girl) demon. After vampires and werewolves, demons are probably the hottest evil supernatural hunk out there (since, if you may recall, the yummy hunky fairy folk Mercurians or Moon-Lunarians are intentionally lying low, or have gone completely under the radar).

Why do we love the bad alpha-boys and the bad alpha-girls so much? Is it the illusion of confidence and power that they exude? Is it the careless "cool" attitude? (Because, you know, caring is so uncool.) Is it rebellion against the *status quo* (regardless of the actual nature of the *status quo*)? Aggression pretending to be pure strength? Bravado masquerading as courage—or at least the willingness to dare, to try all kinds of outrageous and extreme things? Pride and attitude? Pride and Prejudice? A Tale of Two Cities? Ahem! The ability to sexually dominate us in bed, and add a little (just enough) safe and consensual pain to heighten our pleasure?

Maybe it's more a reflection on us as a society that we are so stuck in a store-brand ritual rut, so boring and timid and developmentally lazy, that we dream of conflict and trouble, and therefore "look up" to powerful troublemakers? Because seriously, a demon is a terrifying fiend, either disembodied or in the flesh, with or without horns and a tail, and it is *pure unadulterated evil.* How in BLEEPING! BLEEP! is *that* sexy?

Well, let's explore this conundrum. There are in fact quite a few very good reasons for the attraction.

Demons and hence Uranusians are hot (literally and figuratively) not only because they hail from Tartarus, or Hades, or random San Fernando Valley hellholes, but because they seem to have the supernatural ability to come across as the ultimate expert lovers.

And okay, because, there's the tantalizing *possibility of redemption* involved. Oh, how tempting it is, that redemption thing!

According to common lore, demons are nothing more than angels gone bad. In other words, fallen angels. And as such, they didn't always used to be evil.

Demons come in two flavors—

A. The redeemable but currently thoroughly evil asshole demon who is resisting all efforts at salvation, and:

B. The already redeemed former asshole demon who is now on the path to purgatory, but slowly—since he or she is, well, still a demon and not a stampeding hippopotamus.

C. There is no C. There are no permanent "unredeemable" demons, because what would be the fun in that? The secret attraction of evil is that it *can* be fixed.

Both A and B flavor demons are equally sexy, hot, attractive, desirable, and super-powerful to the average mortal—and to so many supernaturals of other persuasions. Pick A or B, depending on your level of challenge, and have a go at it! Sweet redemption!

The planet Uranus is well known for its amazing concentric rings, basically "fields" of orbiting rock garbage and bits of asteroids and other random space stuff that got sucked into Uranus's gravitational field or got expelled outward in some primordial hiccup during its formational period. Sounds familiar? Yup, it's just like your sphincter, after a taco and burrito combo platter "processing" hellfire funfest.

What does it mean to be a demonic Uranusian?

It means that you are obsessed with posturing, and looking up your own asshole, and yes, *you are obsessed with lashing out at others* in the true manner of a jerk. Because you are generally so mean and awful, you are in fact truly *dangerous* to others. Because you are also attractive and handsome and gorgeous and strong—if you want to be— you are even more dangerous. You can make people and supernatural soul mates commit all kinds of horrors, stupidities, and regrettable acts, as you drag them down to hell.

Ideal Mate for a Uranusian

An ideal mate for you is probably another asshole demon. Or, at least, that's what many would like to say to you, after being screwed over by you so thoroughly.

However, let's be honest, even at your sneakiest "best," you are not the best fit for some people.

For example, a **Jupiterian** zombie is thoroughly unsatisfying as a romantic partner. At best you can enter their poor rotting flesh and possess them, forcing them to do the Dance of the Sugar Plum Fairy (or fae!) in a mauve tutu while lurching about on the street. But the amusement factor will quickly exhaust itself, as you quickly realize that there is nothing funny or fun about inhabiting a broken bloated corpse. Blech! They would never even know you're in there, as they sit around and chow down on some poor victim's brains. How uber-lame!

Vampire **Venusians** can be exciting for a while, since the two of you are so much alike. But eventually they will not tolerate you either possessing them or trying to date them, so there will be blood. Neither yours nor theirs, naturally, but *someone's* blood. And then the two of you drama queens will walk in opposite directions, your black leather outerwear flapping in the wind.

Neither will faerie (fairies fae fey) **Mercurians** or **Moon-Lunarians** be likely to take your sh*—BLEEP! for long. They are far too sophisticated, smart, and powerful to be tempted by you. They are also far too cool-hearted to care to redeem you. And as for any attempts at corporeal possession, you can get your own asshole handed back to you on a magic stick. So, just keep your distance from Faerie.

Earthlings are, on the other hand, a delightfully brief true love-match. You will gleefully consume them, break their heart, and give them the best one-night stand of their life, before you drag them down to hell . . . except for *that one* very special Earthling. The one who will insinuate into your evil heart and fill your wicked soulless echo-chamber, and suddenly, BAM! You remember what it is *to love*, and you are *redeemed!* Noooooo!

Another excellent supernatural love match for the demon asshole is its polar opposite—the ghostly angel **Quantum Planetoid**. Just as a demon's sole purpose is to corrupt, the angel's is to redeem and save. Send an angel after a demon, and there will not be blood, but there will likely be plenty of poop and feathers flying, until either the angel succeeds, or the demon succeeds, depending on who is stronger. Our bet is on the angel, because this is, after all, a *love* match.

Asteroid Belt, Oort Cloud, and Pluto—Your Ghost Angel Lover

The most ephemeral supernatural lover is a ghost or an angel. Most recently, angels have become a hot commodity in the media supernatural lust object category. Often they tend to be portrayed with a whiff of the "fallen angel" about them, with gray or even black wings (basically looking like military black ops commandos with buzz haircuts, ammo belts, and yes, those *wings* vaguely sticking out from the back . . . or being blown about like vaporous hallucinations born of three martinis), so the lines between angel and demon get kind of super-blurred. But just as often, the good angels are allowed to remain on the heavenly side. And as such, they are a powerful force in popular entertainment. Also, they have these really big, gorgeous, fluffy-bunny white wings which then get emulated by underwear runway models. . . .

Here, fortunately you are on the healthy side of the obsession. If someone *must* be in love with a supernatural winged entity, let it be one on the side of Good. Because the other side is basically crazy.

Ghosts on the other hand, are more in the gray area, and can be of either persuasion. They are disembodied and intriguing, and they can blow their lover's mind. That is, the lover is in bed alone, and they think they are getting . . . ahem . . . *blown*.

Angels are the warriors of heaven, sent to maintain the balance on earth. Ghosts are those of the dead who have chosen not to pass on for some reason. Yeah, they are two different things entirely. But in the formation of a Quantum Planetoid supernatural personality, we've mashed them together, to create an interesting ephemeral hybrid.

The Asteroid Belt is full of small planetoid heavenly bodies, and Pluto is one similar object, and the Oort Cloud is the farthest thing in the solar system and it's just some random space sh**—BLEEP! and fart gases, and sure, there are comets and meteors and asteroids in there, all in a cosmic soup. It's vague and uncertain, and—just like angels and ghosts—sort of, kind of, *there*.

So what does it mean to be a Quantum Planetoid?

It means that *you are obsessed with doing the right thing*, and you are obsessed with all kinds of vague lost causes, as you flit about in your gas clouds on heavenly wings.

Ideal Mate for a Quantum Planetoid

The answer should not be all that surprising. Anyone and everyone in the supernatural soul mate hierarchy can make an okay match with these guys and gals, because angels and ghosts are mutable and all-permeating, and they are (like lint and cat hair) frigging everywhere. (And because they have the patience and perseverance and stickiness of, well, saints and lint and cat hair.)

However, we're not aiming for just an okay match, we want the best.

So, who's the best love match for these airborne creatures of goodness and light?

Why, **Earthlings**, of course. They are the most fulfilling and affectionate combination for angels, and they are certainly nostalgia-buckets for ghosts. Furthermore, they are such a *relief*—after trying to love and cherish bloodless corpses, oozing brains, dry bones, or random demonic tentacles.

Because after long-suffering eons of doing the right thing—cleaning up body rot, burying body parts, wiping assholes, sweeping away clumps of fur, stuffing ancient rags, scrubbing away stubborn bloodstains, redeeming windbags—these fine creatures deserve simple uncomplicated love.

And chocolate!

Or at least that fresh coffee *aroma* at the bookstore café.

The Supernatural Matchmaker's General Advice to Soul Mates— The Love Secret

Notice that we have not mentioned or attempted to classify endless other supernatural soul mate possibilities—elves, mermaids (pardon, mer-people), dragons, golems, minotaurs, gnomes, lamias, chimeras, space blobs, et cetera.

It is simply not possible. Nor is it practical. There are an infinite number of entities that could be your (or each other's) supernatural soul mate.

What we have given you are the *hottest paranormal love commodities* in *this solar system*. Our own solar system.

There are many, many, many, many (times many) other solar systems, and they all have planets, and those planets have distinctive names and personalities and *souls* honoring their cultural traditions. Really, they would not even make sense to us! (Nor should they.)

I mean, if someone told you that a **Blargoid** snoofle makes a wonderful supernatural soul mate for a **X'Froidalite** choochoohar ... or that the telepathic powers of the **Goidusar** drapplequi make it an unsuitable suction unit connection or soul mate for a **Srorrrrdyx** tradliia because of their teleporting third follicle xdufgul, you would not be particularly thrilled. Nor would you be in any way enlightened.

So take an experienced, wise supernatural matchmaker's word on this—it's a big universe, and there's plenty to go around, and plenty in your own little corner.

How then do you attract your very own supernatural soul mate?

Easy!

Simply *be yourself.*

And now, for that secret love advice. Yes, that one, the one true *love secret.*

The Love Secret

Love is all around you. Don't look for it, don't reminisce about it, don't wait too long, don't waste your life (or undeath) in search of it.

*Instead, recognize the secret truth that **love itself is supernatural**.*

Worlds expand, veils are cast aside, wings flap open and unfurl dramatically, fur shines more glossy, fangs disappear, brainy gray matter oozes in meaningful patterns. You no longer require corrective lenses. Everything becomes clear and sure and easy . . . when you *love*.

And now you know.

So, shoo! What are you waiting for? Go and get yourself some of that supernatural goodness!

That bookstore café around the corner is officially open.

Just let go of that fire escape.

About the Author

Vera Nazarian is a two-time Nebula Award® Finalist and a member of Science Fiction and Fantasy Writers of America. She immigrated to the USA from the former USSR as a kid, sold her first story at 17, and has been published in numerous anthologies and magazines, honorably mentioned in Year's Best volumes, and translated into eight languages.

Vera made her novelist debut with the critically acclaimed *Dreams of the Compass Rose,* followed by *Lords of Rainbow.* Her novella *The Clock King and the Queen of the Hourglass* made the 2005 Locus Recommended Reading List. Her debut collection *Salt of the Air* contains the 2007 Nebula Award-nominated "The Story of Love." Recent work includes the 2008 Nebula Finalist novella *The Duke in His Castle,* science fiction collection *After the Sundial* (2010), *The Perpetual Calendar of Inspiration* (2010) and three Jane Austen parodies, *Mansfield Park and Mummies* (2009), *Northanger Abbey and Angels and Dragons* (2010), *Pride and Platypus: Mr. Darcy's Dreadful Secret* (2012), and *Pagan Persuasion: All Olympus Descends on Regency* (forthcoming), all part of her *Supernatural Jane Austen Series.*

After many years in Los Angeles, Vera now lives in a small town in Vermont. She uses her Armenian sense of humor and her Russian sense of suffering to bake conflicted pirozhki and make art.

In addition to being a writer, philosopher, and award-winning artist, she is also the publisher of Norilana Books.

Official website:
www.veranazarian.com